sleepers get dreams

sleepers get dreams

ILLREADY

iUniverse, Inc.
Bloomington

sleepers get dreams

iUniverse books may be ordered through booksellers or by contacting:

iUniverse
1663 Liberty Drive
Bloomington, IN 47403
www.iuniverse.com
1-800-Authors (1-800-288-4677)

ISBN: 978-1-4620-1288-6 (sc)
ISBN: 978-1-4620-1289-3 (ebk)

Printed in the United States of America

iUniverse rev. date: 04/28/2011

To my friends: The life of a writer can get very solitary, and I thank every one of you who supported me. You all know who you are, and I hope to be a better friend as we move forward.

Sincerely,
Jamil Robbins

Pain

He sat there as tears rushed down like his face
was a football field. His body shook like a leaf on a windy day.
His self-worth was as shallow as a baby pool. His mind was as trapped as an inmate. Inside,
he was beating himself up like he had idle hands. Love had abandoned him as if it didn't
want 'im. He leaned on depression like elation haunted him. He tapped his foot like it was
uncontrollable. He lost his family and kids like they were portable, and his voice was never
audible. He wiped his face and began to pace as frustration and fear crawled and chased. His
heart beat like choir drums; everything he desired now was won. He turned the bottle of
Prozac like a thermostat. Then he lay on his back, waiting to gain freedom from the pain.

One Chance

I'm looking for it, but I can't grasp it.
Maybe I need Top Shelf Wine, a blanket, and
a picnic basket. It might be hard to find, but I'll
still keep searchin'; maybe I'm off the wall, but
I want it for certain. Maybe a bouquet of roses,
delivered; the thought makes my heart shiver.
I'm burning for this, the consequences will be
so great, so I think it's worth the risk. Maybe
kindness or maybe fancy dining. Passionate
kissing and sharing food. Maybe then I can't
lose. I'm going to tie up these fancy shoes
and ask her to dance. Then maybe, slowly
but surely, I'll get that one chance.

Beautiful

Beautiful you are in so many ways.
I'm blessed to have seen you for so
many days. Your smile brightens up
the earth from thousands of miles away.
You are the one who gets things done.
I will always stick with you 'cause
your beauty is a role model. You are
the definition of beautiful,
like blue and yellow-purple
hills, Harriet Tubman freeing slaves, and Barack Obama the
president. Even in the dark,
I can see your glow. That's
why you are beautiful.

If

If tomorrow never comes,
what will you do today? Will
you do evil things or will you
sit and pray? Will you rush destiny
or will you sit and cry? Will you
have faith in eternal life or will
you just wanna die? If the devil
takes you underground for eternity,
will you accept it or call on Jesus?
The devil will grant you all your
wishes as long as whatever God
says, you don't believe in it. As angels
play harps, you will only hear scratching
chalkboards. Until you say, "Devil, take
me. I can't take no more!" He helps
you, then he breaks you down. Until
you crawl. So saying "if" is like
having no faith at all.

Only The Strong Survive

It's amazing how we take life for granted.
When our time here is so short, we emphasize and
worry about things we can't change, we indulge in
things that waste our precious time, and we look up
one day and our time is up, and we thought
it would never be us. We begin asking a person who we
don't even know for forgiveness and mercy. We all have
no choice but to surrender when it's time. Why are you
crying? You knew all your life it was coming, you just
didn't know when. There was no way you could have prevented it, and now you want
another life after death when you didn't
appreciate the first one. Who are you, God?

Lost in Time

Where am I? This isn't my world. I just wanna
curl up like a child. Where am I, with these
diverse expressions, and everyone I talk to is
stressin'? Birds flock of the same feather,
so I'd rather leave. They won't let me,
but I'll escape, then someone will believe I need help
when they see the yellow tape from wall to wall.
It's misery, and all in all I'm missing me, so I'll hide to
cage the rage in me. Up and down like a seesaw; ain't
nobody brave like me from triumph to tragedy. I faced nothing but
agony, so for now I'm blind, but one day
I'll shine for being lost in time.

Why You Are Precious

You are one of God's forgiving children. You listen to
others when you're having a bad day, and when others
are living a bad way, you still see the good in them.
You encourage with a push so you can create
strength and pull them in. You realize life is bigger
than just
you. You accept trials and tribulations 'cause you know there is a greater
place than earth. You're humble, but you know
your worth. You're beautiful because of your courage
and strength. You're always willing to go the length
and width of your full potential, and you know you
will forever be a friend, so rare a treasure beyond
compare. You uplift, you hold together, you smile,
you help others walk that extra mile. You listen
more than you talk, but when you do talk, it's as soothing
as Epsom salt, so people stop hoping to learn a lesson
because you're the opposite of depressing. You feed on
faith so your doubt can starve to death. That's why you
are precious.

Have Mercy

Have mercy on me, Lord, and take this pain away from
me. Lord spare me guilt, humility, and anger.
Lord have mercy on my soul. Forgive me for my
wrongdoing, for I didn't realize how my consequences
and actions affected my peers. Have mercy on me, Lord;
believe that I'm a good person. Have faith in me like I
have had it in you. Have mercy on me, Lord, and lift this
confusedness from me.
Give me a sense of direction, for I am lost.
Have mercy on me, Lord, 'cause no one else has.
Have mercy on me, Lord
Have mercy on me, Lord
Have mercy on me, Father
I'm at the point of no return, and I need you to listen
to my actions because I'm past talking.

Strive

I've written all day until my hands hurt.
I've put my goal and ambition to work.
I transform in freestyle battles; the emotions almost
make me cry. I bring it from the heart and soul as my
temperature rises. My pencil is my fist and the paper
is my punching bag. I swing harder than life until I
crash like Larenz Tate; turn on a beat and my mind races
like an interstate. My punch lines are like George
Foreman's. I'll eat ya plate. It's so much feeling that it's
like therapy some days. I got on my knees and asked
freestyle to marry me. I'm on a natural high, and it gives
me the chills. I can't imagine me getting on a stage and
standing still. Anger makes me dance and holler as the
messages grab everybody up in the collar. I'm
chewing the pursuing for acknowledgment that I'm
the best until the best tells me I'm the best and there's
something better than selling crack; until then, I'll keep
striving for that contract.

Make Sense

I'm striving for sense, but I'm not stupid, and being locked
up will make you feel useless. Who are you to judge? We're all
searching for the promised land. I'll have more needs when
I'm out than I had when I was in, 'cause I'm leaning on
a threshhold of a new start and the beginning is the end. My
patience is wearing thin. I'm staying calm, trying to swallow
my pride, but the thought of the future got me feeling dead
wrong. I don't need nobody to help me do my time, or even
speak to me. I'm as isolated in here as I am on the streets. Can't
trust a soul if I want to meet my goal. My mind don't get
along with my heart, so I'm fighting with life, broken promises,
and negative results. Pacing around until the tension halts. So
why shouldn't I take a mile out of an inch,
because if I don't fight, it won't make sense.

I Want You to Know

I want you to know that talk is cheap. I want you
to know actions speak louder than words. I want
you to know if you don't stand for something, you will
fall for anything. I want you to know that you have to take
the bitter with the sweet. I want you to know that things that
seem dull sometimes shine brightly. I want you to know that everything that
glitters ain't gold. I want you to know that we are all
in an hourglass, so have as much fun as you can before
your time passes. Don't you realize that I want you
to know?

Up to Me

I venerate life and vow to be loyal. I yearn
to fight wicked temptations even if I've failed.
Obstacles were obscured, but I plan to prevail
with propriety. I will not be enticed by games that street punks
play. I will learn from my peers' mistakes. I will be perfect
in life: abstinent, sober, God fearing, and humble. You
don't have to believe me. It's up to me; don't worry about why I
haven't
conquered my goals. I've tried being oblivious of the oddity
that life is not up to me.

Rescue Me

SOS I'm suffering because I'm waiting on somebody
else, and I'm holding my breath until they come. SOS
I need help. I have a pounding headache and pain medicine
isn't working, so I'm waiting on somebody else, and I'm
holding my breath until they come rescue me. I'm
stranded, waiting on somebody else, and I'm holding my
breath until they come. I've just been shot, and I'm waiting on somebody else, and I'm
holding my breath until they come. My fingertips are blue, my face is pale,
my legs are shaking. I release my lungs and exhale; my
eyes close. 'Cause I waited on somebody else. I died saying, "Rescue me."

Turning Me Around

The worst things can make the best out of you.
You vow never to go through again what brought tears
to drip from your chin. Some work good under
pressure. It's like standing on stage and being tormented by a heckler. Prepare for
the end while some shake it off and fight for the win.
What heats me up is knowing that it's never enough, and what
geeks me up is knowing that I can't give up on
myself, instead of life. I sometimes don't know my
own strength until I talk to Christ, and he assures
me he will take care of everything, so I brush my
shoulders off and wait for my wings, but the only
anticipation I possess is picking up my son and never putting him down, and that goal is
what's
turning me around.

I Don't

I don't have to get your
opinion, it's how I feel about it.
I don't have to ask if I got my own.
I don't have to listen if I know it all.
I don't have to be bothered with anyone
if I stay in the house. I don't have to ride
the bus if I hitch a ride. I don't even have
to like the person if they don't give me
a ride. I don't have to be humble. I don't
have to accept losses. I don't have to
accept anything. I don't have to wear
socks and shoes. I don't have to pay
any dues. Grand mama
always told me a hard head makes a
soft ass. Yeah, I got an answer
for everything. I don't
respect myself. So why should I respect you? I don't have to wear condoms. Now I have
AIDS. And I don't understand.

Length

Because I'm sable, they assume I'm
rebellious. But my sturdiness keeps me
serene from oppression. All my life I've
been lashed from turmoil and obstacles.
This is the time to wake up and toil
instead of being prone to the easy way out.
Feeding are frailties. I am fain to take
the initiative to shake the intricacies.
Where were you? When everyone was
sticking together and I was outnumbered. Caught up in haughtiness
that's where you were. Too much pride
for your own good. But scornful
toward your own kind. Feeling
like the fight was insurmountable.
Given up instead of clenching on
to strength. So I'm going to pray for you. For being languorous
to going the length.

Too Late

I didn't listen now I'm rushing through time, There
were clues, but I paid them no mind. The clock won't
rewind and it won't wait. Now I can't control my own
fate. I haven't talked to her in a month's time. It is way
overdue. I'm running down blocks now with one shoe
heavy, panting, and cold sweats. But I'll be damned if I
slow down even though my head is spinning. 'Cause what goes around comes around.
Guilt and depression are part of the reason.
Now I'm holding onto a gate with extensive wheezing.
But it's worth the fight to see her smile again. I made it
to the steps and begin to grin. I raced into a big white
and red house. I felt like my heart had turned inside out,
and I began to get irate as I held her head in my hand. I
hugged her face, but I realized I was too late.

Things Have Changed

Roses used to blossom, now they wither. Paper hearts
float to the floor, and there's blood on the scissors.
Love's an apple crawling with bugs; it used to be heaven-sent
now ever since it's been rain. Hands and feet shackled
in chains. Milk and honey to chewed liver. Shoulders are
so cold the whole room shivers. Abandoned feelings
in the land of the lost. Things used to be sweet as applesauce, now
things are so gloomy. It's strange and it
saddens me that things have changed.

Tell Me

Tell me something I don't know. I'm not here for your
amusement. I'm not here for a show. I'm here to help my
people break down a wall like Brewster Place. They're not
used to this place. I can see it in their face. I need power so I
need knowledge, so when we break the chains and run free
like wild Indians, we can form an alliance like the Gideon's. Tell me something good like
Chaka Kahn, 'cause all I hear is negativity but with knowledge
they'll never get rid of me. The only way I can teach is by
learning. That's the only thing that keeps the fire inside of me
glistening and burning.

Blame Yourself

Why is it the police officer's fault you got caught? You
thought you were bad enough to taunt. Why is it your baby mama's
fault that you are broke? Didn't you help create that child? Are
you not proud of your accomplishment? Why is it your teacher's
fault that you didn't pass? You didn't even study. Why is
it the probation officer's fault that you're getting revoked? You
surrounded yourself with negativity. Why is it the lifeguard's
fault that the boy drowned? He knew he couldn't swim,
but jumped in twelve feet. Why is it the US soldier's fault
that he shot a nine-year-old Iraqi boy in the chest? The boy was aiming an AR-15 assault
rifle. Why is it God's fault you're
getting nothing but bad luck? You make the bed you lie in.
Do you understand what I'm sayin'? Look in the mirror and
take responsibility for your own actions and send excuses
a packin'.

Happy

Why am I smiling? My days are usually gloomy. I lay
in the bed all day, trapped in four corners. As the agony that's
dragging me becomes unruly, I ask myself, "Why me?" as medicines
flow through an IV. I'm usually more angry than sad as I reach over
and change my colostomy bag. My hands shake like washing machines,
and my voice isn't audible. All I can do is point. No one comes to see
me anymore, and I'm in too deep to reach for shore. I can't tell night
from day, and I often fight to stay awake. I can't envision a future, just
the light above my head. My body winced and someone began to
wave. He repeatedly hollered out, "My brother, you're saved!" Then
my stomach began feeling nourished like I had just been fed. Just
then I realized why I was smiling: 'cause I was dead.

Once Hoped For

The thought of her is like falcons soared by piccolos,
solid gold roses and platinum mistletoes, relaxing on tropical
islands under canopies, watching coastal waters and throwing seaweed at the manatees, or
walking through beaches covered
in diamonds as we watch the sunset over the shore of Thailand.
Seeing her gets me through my miserable day. Now I'm panicking
'cause she hasn't come my way. Did I oversleep or did she change
her mind? Did I just lose track of time? I pray that I haven't
lost my reason to go on. Nothing in this world amounts to her.
If I went mute, I would still try to shout to her. It may be impossible
for me to get the key to this door. I'm content as long as she
knows. She is among the things I once hoped for.

If You Was Me

If you was me, you wouldn't have made it past nine
years old. I'm not measuring your strength, but miles has
been taken out of my one inch. Did you have to take care
of two babies at eight years old? Ma gone for weeks. Leaving only
beets to eat. Did you have to watch the police beat up
Ma then offer you a Snickers bar? If you was me, you would
have given up on catching hope, 'cause it was so far. Have you
ever had to fight grown men at eight years old to keep them
from attacking your mama? Watching blood pour from her
head from drama. Fuck jail. Have you ever had the streets
put you under arrest! Having nowhere to turn, 'cause Ma
was killed from a knife to the chest. Have you ever had an
alcoholic daddy who made promises he couldn't keep?
Out of five boys, Grand mama had only given three somewhere
to sleep. Watching tears run down their checks as social services
slowly drove away. If you was me, you wouldn't have made it past eight
'cause you would have tried to escape to hide way in the troubled
world. Only four remain out of the five boys, no Daddy, no Mama, twenty-two,
twenty-three, twenty-eight, and thirty-one years old. If you was me, you would have realized
that the
world is so cold.

You Can't Hold Water

Some things are better left unsaid, and you acting acquiesce with the feds you want your
freedom and the codefendants to your full of corruptness and cupidity your cowardliness
is going to kill people including yourself you can never get love and respect 'cause no one
condones double crossing
no one wants to be your friend you're an outcast everywhere you go it's dirty looks and
people breaking out like rash you
sold your freedom to the devil so you're confined on the streets
the rest of your life walking through a desert thirsty, because you can't hold water.

Forgive Me

I never knew it would turn out like this. I never meant to run my mouth about shit. They
had me cornered, and I didn't know
what to do. It was either you or me, and I was scared to give up the rest of my life. We played
in sandboxes together, learned about everything together. When Daddy wasn't around, all we
had was us. Now that you're gone, I can't even trust things, things that play back in my mind
now that I'm on the streets and you're doing time. My heart is full
of regret and sorrow 'cause you're forever upset, and I can't
face tomorrow, so I'm putting this barrel in my mouth and
ending my life 'cause I snitched on my brother and got him life.

What Is It?

Is it the clothes I wear or is it the timing that makes you not care? Or is it because you're scared when God is telling you I'm rare? Is it because you are afraid to lose, or because you are afraid to win? Is it the grin, is it a gift and a curse, or just a gift? Maybe just a curse, because there's only one-way left and that's up. It has already been worse. Is it because I get up and do the same thing every day or the way I look? I say it is because you're scorn, or you assume I have horns, or because I picked a rose out of someone else's garden just for you. Is it because you care what other people think, or do you believe I'm out of sync? Is it not worth having to angle your life 'cause I take the risk of losing the angel God has brought into my life. Talk is cheap. I only wish from the deepest part of my heart that I could live it. Until then, I'll keep wondering, What Is It?

Don't You See Me?

I'm inches away from my last breath. Don't you see
me? I'm at the bottom of the lake tangled in seaweed. I raised my hand once and no one
answered, so I began fighting something I
couldn't change. I looked up and I saw the sun, so I raised my hand
again thinking the victory was won, but no one answered so I began to think it was the end,
and I went back to fighting things I couldn't change again, so on my last breath, I didn't
bother to raise my hand. I
said my life is over, bring on the band so God reached down and grabbed me and said, "Oh,
you faithless boy, why didn't you pray?
Next time, believe me, 'cause there's only so many times I will ask you
don't you see me?"

What Do I Do?

What do I do in this trying time when all my time has
been spent? What do I do when I see my brother falling face first and
there is nothing I can do? I pray. What do I do when the world is
getting the best of me, and I wanna wrap a noose around my neck?
I pray. What do I do when the Lord is calling me, and I don't know
how to answer? I pray. What do I do when he takes somebody
close to me? I pray. What do I do when I know tomorrow ain't
promised to me? I pray. What do I do when prayer is no longer
enough? Let God remind you. It's what do he do not what do
I do.

No Regrets

You wonder why I'm antisocial: 'cause you got nothing
to say worth listening to. Your money can't get you into heaven.
And the things you venerate may make you feel like you're in heaven,
but you're not really there. You're sleepwalking if you think the things
you're willing are going to get you something. When all it's doing is
taking from you. The little sense you have left got you trapped in an
illusion. You don't know the real from the fake anymore. Being
brainwashed by others that're brainwashed. You think you're so
smart, but you stay lost and have the nerve to give directions. So
keep the small talk and jokes, 'cause, I'm serious about life. Give
me some space, and I'll give you respect, and I vow that there
will be no regrets.

Never Leave

I would hate for this opportunity to dwindle. If the flame
went out, I would give my blood, sweat, and tears to rekindle it. The
sight of her elevates my spirits. Sometimes when she walks away,
I glance to see if she has wings and a halo. It's like gliding through
riding ocean waves on a dolphin, a diamond in a bowl of pearls, or a rose
in a field of dandelions. The thought of her is like reflections of
sun rays in drops of rain. She's as precious as a leprechaun's pot
of gold. I dream of us sipping Piña Coladas on a beach and holding
hands till we're old. If I could, I would bring her the stars and the
moon
in an attempt to give her the world. I would give her my heart so she
could have all my love. I would give her my eyes so she could see
what God sent me from above. I would parachute from the highest
mountain to get her to believe. Then I would hug her tight and ask
her never to leave.

I Deserve

Maybe I deserved for my mama to abandon my four brothers and me for crack cocaine.
Maybe I deserved to watch my two homies get
shot by an Asian gang. Or maybe I deserved to have stuck-up kids run in my grand mama's
house and hit me with a
pistol. Or maybe I deserved to have another friend get shot
dead in front of my grand mama's house. Or maybe I deserved
to have my brother's car run into a tree and kill him instantly.
Or maybe I deserved to watch my dad fight my ma and throw
our house keys on top of a building. Maybe I deserved to have
my grand mama go through brain surgery and lung cancer. If
I learned anything, it was one valuable lesson. I deserve
God's blessing.

They Don't Love They Self

Why do you think they soulful and rebellious and hollering out it
ain't shit you can tell us? Because they don't love themselves
they feel indifferently about themselves cause deep down inside
they oppress to make themselves feel like there imperfections aren't that bad they hate them
selves the woman say yuck! so now since
no one likes them they don't give a fuck there out to be biased and belligerent because there
ambitions are to treat any and everything as an adversary there ego is a cracked egg and
what they have endured left them in despair now there defiant and hate the world then their
endeavors to hate fails when they watch their
first born come into the world they become so unconventional
that they disregard there hygiene appearance and or health and
they realize they can't love anybody else because they don't love they self.

Can You Blame Me?

Can you blame me for wanting the finer things? Can you blame me for doing whatever I have to do to get it? Well then, can
you blame me for selling drugs to feed my three-year-old son 'cause the economy isn't designed for a felon to have a good job. Then
can you blame me for being walked over by women when I love and respect women? Can you blame me for being kind and humble toward people? Can you blame me for looking for love in the wrong places when I lack so much of it? Can you blame me for wanting first class when all I ever endured was
poverty? Well, point your finger at me and blame me for not giving up.

You Know You Were Wrong

You know you were wrong, so why did you do it? You must not think that fat meat is greasy. Chitterlings are pig intestines (all the stool is passed through). The filthiest part of the pig was forced to slaves to eat. What was the nastiest thing to eat, slaves turned to something edible, and now it is something African Americans considers a delicacy. You know you were wrong, but we made something out of nothing. You know you were wrong, but we overcame the negativity. You know you were wrong, but you were addicted to sin so I forgive you. If you knew better, you would do better. We're not on this earth long, so do yourself a favor and admit when you know you were wrong.

To an Island

My heart has been driven and there was no return. From the point
I was driven, she was as sweet as taffy, and I wanted to be close to her. Her presence gave
my body tremors, her smile was so adequate my emotions simmered. I look away but I can't
help but to stare. If I go to heaven, I know you would be there. I dream of holding you and
kissing your neck. Being away from you keeps me vex. When I don't see you, I suffer, and it's
hard to be patient. Your love is as sacred as the last supper, and I long to be adjacent to your
heart. So I'm following my intuition. I'm better at taking what I think I deserve rather than
receiving what life freely offers. You keep me smilin' so let's get passports and run away to an
island.

Fighting for What You Want

My heart has been confiscated, leaving love conveyed.
I have to cop you no matter what's courted. I'm in a dead run,
hands outstretched to grasp her as I retorted. "Don't give up
on me. I'll always be there!" But she kept a look of despair.
She left my feelings more ill than influenza. My legs didn't feel
boisterous. My ambitions were held captive, and I suddenly
felt omitted 'cause she was indifferent. Her love was obscured.
What I had endured made me want to hide the hurt with
chauvinistic comments. I leaned over and began to vomit.
Suddenly, I picked my head up and lurched, 'cause her smile
was luminous. The connection was as potent as a magnet
in a nail factory. She smiled and whispered, "I'm glad you
came after me."

Goosebumps and Butterflies

I hate good-bye, 'cause I may never see you again. In order
to begin, you have to accept that there's an end. Nothing lasts
forever, but we pretend. Afterward, we still have a hard time
accepting it. I remember what it felt like when I first lost love.
I was devastated. It was nowhere to be found, and I vowed to
never let love come back again. I didn't want to deal with it
anymore. My heart broke as if love had hands. I tried to piece it
back together, but it ran for cover. You don't miss a good thing until it's gone.
I don't speak about love anymore, even when I'm alone, but I often scowl
at it with tears in my eyes, 'cause love gives me goosebumps and butterflies.

Keep Ya Head Up

After all you have been through, why is your head down? You are the strongest person I know. Don't give up and drown now. Swim to land where there's sunny days, palm trees, umbrella drinks, and sand. Where there are no worries, and you're not blind to the facts, and your future isn't blurry. Why is your head down because of things you can't change? Making things more difficult, driving you insane. Run through the rain until the sun comes out and shines again. Keep believing that you can win a minor setback for a major comeback. Everything you lost, God will give back. Search for the land of milk and honey. Stay focused, because life isn't funny, there's something bigger than money and freedom, so when they tell you that you ain't nothing, don't believe 'em. Get up, because the sky's the limit, and you have to keep ya head up.

The Truth

When I hear your voice, I wake up out of a deep sleep
and smile. It's like an aurora created by God that leaves an aureole above your head. I
emulate my life to impress you. I employ myself to meeting your expectations, because I
want to love you. I don't know if it's fate, but losing you has made me emaciate. So being
without you is unhealthy. I consider you my troubles, which makes you my pure joy, because
I know the Holy Spirit is testing my faith, which lets me know that I'm closer to being where
I want to be and that's with you and that's the truth.

Dream

My dreams are vivid. I had a fantasy and you were in it. Things that we did would have been better if we had lived it. The love is unimaginable, bonded by God, doing work you love now that's a great job. Getting paid with the sight of her if temptation was a women there's no doubt I'll have a fight with her. I might need a ref. I love this fantasy like I love my last breath. My hands outstretched, I beckoned to her, but she didn't move, so I started steppin' to her 'cause this I didn't want to lose. I shouted we would make a strong team, then God said make a choice then a light beamed. I said if loving her is wrong, I don't wanna be right. Then I woke up in a cold sweat and realized it was a dream.

Fighting Time

You're weary of being ridiculed. You're ready to sacrifice your freedom by murdering a slew of people. The sassiness lets me know you're undaunted. You're scuffling because you're stout and soulful about biased people. You defy judgmental folk, who deride to make themselves feel better about their frailties to attain ambitions. You must eliminate the abhorrence and let your mind fight, because we are all fighting time.

What I Offered

My hands are in my pockets, but I can't feel a thing. My chest feels hollow without it. I show it often, but today I can't find it.

I'm perspiring with the thought of not having it. She will be disappointed if I lost it, but I'm nervous about rejection. Temptation is telling me to try anyway, but first I have to locate something. I can hear it beating a mile a minute. Just then, the beat got softer, so I grabbed her hand and smiled, 'cause I could feel what I offered.

Thank You

Mama,

Thank you for lovin' that crack daddy. Thank you for lovin' your gin, grand mama. Thank you for takin' me in. I'm stronger 'cause of sin. My hurt is gone; might be the reason I win. I'm sure for some, it'll be a shot to the chin. But I'm turnin' my back to the wind. I gotta gauntlet to attend. The straightforward going straight through, so instead of fuck you, it's thank you.

ILLREADY.

All I Know

All I know is selling crack, ain't a fuckin' soul who got my back. What am I supposed to do, lay down and fucking die? I got chronic preexisting health reasons and can't even pay for my prescriptions. Ain't nobody giving me shit for free. So fuck the police and fuck your judgmental mutha-fuckas, 'cause I gotta go, 'cause my three-year-old hungry and Mama can't get no money. So, I'm walkin' in these Jordans until you can see my toe. Ain't nothin' like fast money, so sellin' crack is all I know.

F.E.A.R. M.O.N.E.Y. entertainment
PRESENTS
WORMWOOD
by
ILLREADY

I Need 2 Know

Chorus: I need to know are you my savior
'cause if you are, I need a favor.
I been pointed out by my neighbors.
God, if you don't get me now, then
get me later.

Verse 1:
Blessed is the man who don't walk ungodly.
Jesus, rebuke the devil out of my body;
do not leave my soul in destitution.
I pled for relief when there was no substitute.
When my spirit was overwhelmed, I swallowed
my pride and asked for help. 'Cause he's the
only one who felt the pain that I felt.

Verse 2:
I didn't know where else to turn. I was tired of living.
There was no way to modify the way I was feeling.
I couldn't accept the things that I couldn't change.
My heart was weary; I felt God was playing games.
I'm tired of suffering. God, where the hell are you?
I'm fighting for some faith, but God, it's hard to do.

You Mean the World 2 Me

Chorus: You mean the world 2 me I would put my life
on the line for you.
You mean the world 2 me I made it through
the storm so I can shine for you.
I say wherever you at, I'll be there.
I say wherever you at, I'll be there.

Verse 1:
You gone need more than a plunger 'cause ain't shit
movin' you in the same position as last year, so what is you
provin'. My flow conflagration so congeal the illusion.
No need for confirmation, I know you feel the conclusion.
But me, I need far more sipping martini's on a yacht like a
commodore. With a Brazilian in a bikini whose body's contour.
You feel me! Puffin' Cubans with foreigners get stock pointers
y'all niggards still hangin' on blocks and corners. Went from
makin' choices that was bringing me down to my niggards
telling me I deserve the crown. The chains are off. I'm getting
paid for gaining my thoughts. Any niggard who wants it gets
turned to a grain of salt. This ain't the Mickey Mouse Club.
You boys are goofy. We living lavish with the mini bar right by
the Jacuzzi. Toasting shots of ace of spade with a gorgeous
floozy.

Y'all settle for anything like a damn hobo, Ya boy
aiming high like Tony Romo in Costa Rica sippin'
margaritas with a heartthrob sharin' marinated
ribs and corn on the cob. Under a canopy
throwing seaweed at the manatees as we watch the coastal
waters she's trying hard to be a tease. But ain't no other place
she rather be, but on this island every time our eyes contact,
she can't stop smilin'. Ain't no way I wouldn't go hard for a
feeling like this baby so appealing, I can't stop reachin' for
a kiss. I told her 'bout my dreams and my plans to ball
'bout, rockin' a big crowd at Carnegie Hall she put her hand
on my back and said before you walk you gotta crawl then
she told me 'bout her dreams to quit her job at the mall.

Verse 3:
Baby, look. I'm so into you some good had to come out of
all the bullshit I been through. The game is faulty
and niggards is salty, let me make this last run then we
can leave Milwaukee. Boo. I know you against it, but
we gotta catch it fast. We never get out of here
sittin' on our ass. I wanna give you whatever you
ask, enjoy every moment. You know, making it last.
Sightseeing in Paris and taking pictures by the
Eiffel Tower I can see marriage being too sweet
to go sour. Man! I can see our babies throwing
flowers. Yeah, I can see *dat*! It's some gas in
the car, okay gimme kiss I'll be back. Three hours
flat everything went smooth, and then
I heard break youself, and I took a deep breath. All of a sudden
I felt death then I said to myself, "Damn! We should
of left."

Breakdown

Hopped in the two doe pulling out like new growth
mama gotta kulo`she eyeing papi chulo. Baby don't
deprive me of none of that. Ride me with that fat-fat ass goin'
clap-clap. I'm the choice between them other cats. They like
watching paint dry, they ain't fly. But baby, I got wings. I could
take you to heaven. I'll slide you a ring if you're lucky like sevens.

My Whips Bananas

Chorus: My whips bananas my whips whips bananas
my whips bananas my whips whips bananas
(little girl's voice) look at those wheels!
Ain't that nice!

Verse 1:
Whips bananas got 'em all goin' ape eighteen-inch lifts sittin' on
twenty-eights. Candy corn yellow, lookin' moist like cake, she lickin'
her fingers like I'm her choice for today. Flats look stupid big
boy on the Rivi custom deuces on the charger mashing with the
hemi dream-sickle bubble got the Ashanti's through the city
Ninja Turtle cutti sittin' up like a tittie yeah in Milwaukee we
play with them cars cruising through traffic stuntin' like stars
bitches wanna fuck the whip, but they settle for the driver.
She sparking up weed 'cause she can tell I'm a rider.

White lambo look like a bag of sugar paint job
snot and the guts looking booger the davins spinnin' tough you
can call me a looker oh boy the mil very luxurious freaking
like Adina cavalina lookin glorious twenty-six-inch spokes choppin'
like warriors banana bubble eye Benz lookin' so notorious.
Ole school bronco with the monster truck build sittin' on them
thirties damn if looks could kill promethazine yellow with
the chromed-out grill when it comes to them cars nobody
fuckin' with the mill.

Verse 3:

A '74 ole school lac platinum gray with the top knocked
back, swisher rolled tight, got the heater in my lap
hotter than a fever 'bout to strike like a match assassins choppin'
the concrete like an ax whipping like a player till the axle crack
jalapeño magnum with the nacho cheese guts eights so high
when it dips you see the struts. Skylark at the light lookin' like
a bullet gunpowder interior with a hammer watch 'em pull it
rollin' through Motown then Berry Gordy shoes looking magic
on the feet like Dorothy's.

Are You Perfect?

Are you so perfect that you never make a mistake? Does the
highway stop so you can walk across the interstate? Do you look
in the mirror and see no flaws? Do your bowel movements smell like
white diamond? Do you always have perfect timing? Do you play
all sports like a pro? Do you not know what rejection is 'cause no
one has ever told you no? Do you think your schemes are clever?
Can you predict the weather? So why you pointin' out my imperfections? To make yourself
feel better.

Chorus 2x: Are you perfect aha aha aha aha:
Verse 2:
Do you wake up and your breath smell good? Is it always I can
never if I could? Do you always got an answer for everything? Do
they always roll out the red carpet like you a king or queen? Are
you so beautiful that you never have to groom? If the elevator
is packed, do they always make room? Do nothin' you buy ever
have a tax? Are you always first and never last? Do you never have
to give your car some gas? Do you live unhealthy, but stay in good
condition? Every time you have somethin' to say, does everyone
listen? Does God always send you a letter? So why you pointin'
out my imperfections? To make yourself feel better.

Verse 3:
Can you change anything you come across? Do you always have
the directions and never get lost? Was that you they hung on that
cross? Do you never have to work for anything, and everything you
want somebody always brings it to you? Did God break the mold when he
made you? Do people never owe you, but still pay you? Are you
always part of the solution and never the problem? Do people
always look at you and say nobody can stop 'em? Does nothin'
ever fall apart in your life? It's always together, so why you pointin'
out my imperfections? To make yourself feel better.

God is Dead

Chorus 2x: God is dead so I don't wanna be alive.
I wanna be with him, 'cause on earth, I
been deprived.

Verse 1:
Where am I and am I here alone? I'm walking through a desert
with a fear of the unknown. I see abandoned cars with no windshields.
My head is spinnin' like windmills. I'm being followed by black
cats and it's too hot to sit still, but there's a soothing breeze and
my feet keep moving every time I breathe. I don't wanna stay, but
I damn sure don't wanna leave. I gotta good feeling 'bout my
destination from afar. I see familiar faces, ones I been missing
for so many years. I can't fight this feeling. I can't hold back these
tears.

Verse 2:

God is dead; that means death is amazing. I've been suffering for
so long that I was starting to get impatient. I didn't have the nerve
2 pull the trigger, but I was accompanied by misery. The earth was
growing bigger, leaving me lost in history. You can tell me I ain't
tough, but you ain't lived my life. I done had enough. The pain has been
unbearable all my life. The agony been draggin' me, and I'm in need
of a peace of mind. I grasped for a bit of sanity, watching bystanders
feast on time. This is one promise that can't be broken. This journey
is guaranteed. I'm no longer feeling closed in. I broke into a sweat
until I got pale. Oh, my God, this is like central air in hell.

Verse 3:

My chest is hurting and my hands are shakin'. I'm overcome by
sorrow, and I'm feelin' forsaken. I've tried to be strong, but it's
giving me a headache. I've been without love so long that my heart
is feelin' like dead weight. I told my mama I missed her, and then I
hugged my brother. I was crying as I kissed her, feelin' so asunder.
The sun was smiling at us, and we were surrounded by angels. I
couldn't breathe, but it wasn't my asthma. Then I screamed, "God,
I thank you!" Then the angels began to point to an island ahead,
and then I realized why I was smilin': because I was dead.

Prepare 4 War

Hook:
There are some events that nothin' prepares you 4. You're neck deep, so prepare 4 war (repeat 2x). We are all fighting somethin' that we can't kill. The fight is insurmountable, time is real.
(repeat 2x)

Verse 1:

I'm crouched behind a wall with a plot to give it my all. See, I don't know if it sees me, but if I let it get too close, it's gonna leave me, so I'm glancing at other falling soldiers, but I'm still in denial. I'll be damned if I become what I see. This is not a option for me, so I'm reloading, realizing I'm a victim now. I'm army crawling for cover 'cause I see I'm outnumbered. I've just been shot by time.

Breakdown

Operation hourglass, it's a hell of a battle. Yeah, time is moving
fast. I notice I'm hit. I gotta abort this task. I'm insubordinate.
It can kiss my ass. And there are not many left. They're all lost in it.
One day you start, then you're forced to end it. You betta use it
wisely and quit pretendin' 'cause you facin' danger. Quit trippin'.
(repeat 2x)

I'm 'bout my cheese; you can call me a craftsman, you a
has-been. I tossed more bags than a trashman. Your days are
numbered. Just peep the calendars' time and send one clean through
you like a janitor until your legs give way like a compass, now you're drifting like
ocean waves. Sound the trumpet. You ain't about money, ain't shit. Discussed: I'm running
for president, you running for the fuckin' bus. It
blindside you. Time is blizzard, paper hearts float and there's blood
on the scissors. Need is a sign of being weak, so take heed 'cause
it'll catch you while you're taking a leak. It's kinda rough; you ain't smooth at all. You could
lose it all. End of the story that concludes it all. There are some events, but nothing prepares
you for your neck deep, so prepare for war.

Lack of Good Love

I don't know what it is about good love, but it no longer exists
in the land of dying. It abandoned me for so long that I can't stop
crying. Sometimes, I believe that it has feet, 'cause it's always
running away into the street. It's a prisoner of war, but it won't accept defeat. It got
me lost in a race against time. I tried to keep up, but
it left me far behind. I done searched high and low, and it's still
hard to find. I've been severely wounded in this battle. I'm draggin'
through the valley with death's shadow. I'm fightin' as I watch love
sattle lack of good love.

ILLREADY

a*ka*
Lungs

Emcee's betta' practice, 'cause lungs will chop ya head off
like you was John the Baptist.

I made it my own way like Papa Murphy's. I resurrect like it was Easter to bake you turkeys. You ain't even gotta ask me. I'm James worthy. I want the sunny side up, like a bunch of eggs. It's a valuable point in case you missed it. Play animal and catch a bullet in your brisket. Flow so cold, you need ear muffs to listen. Watch me come across the middle like a capital A. Boy, I hold more bars than a soap dish. I done went through more scales than a boat of fish. Every thing I touch is hot, I need oven mitts, man. Y'all end weak like Sunday.

In memory of Brandon and Brenda Robbins
with love, forever.

About the author

Jamil Robbins was raised by his grand mama, Mary L. Hughes, who took him and his four brothers in after their ma abandoned the boys for the love of crack cocaine. She was shortly murdered due to a drug-related issue. To make a long story short, procrastination is an abrupt hindrance to absolute failure. Sleepers get dreams.

I tried to sell dope, but it wasn't a finish line; the girls I had not only drank out of their cup, but finished mine. I thought I was too smart for school, but I didn't know shit. If I knew then what I know now, I would have captured what I set out to get. All my business was unfinished until I had so much on my plate that my dreams were diminished. My eyes were bigger than my belly, and what used to be ambition is now nothing but jelly. I sought advice from those who had been there and done that, and they said they were gone—fought life until their line ran flat. So I made a bet until I was so far in debt that I was like a fish in a net, lost and trapped; and I thought I had it all mapped. There was only one person left to turn to, the only one who could stop hell when it was trying to burn through. But the hell is with you. You ain't gotta believe, but I'm sand. I was facing forty years, but now I'm a free man.

How are you gonna give me directions, if you're lost too?

I used to work for his ass, but he bought you.

I don't owe him shit, but you do. I don't care how much you fight, he ain't gonna get off you. Even when you think it's all right, he gonna cross you, and everything he gave your ass gonna cost you.

I broke into a church and slept by a cross, 'cause even when my bridge was burnt I got across. Everyone I was around was so damn self-centered, and no one was allowed to exit, but they all entered. And when we were at the point of no return and the only option was to sacrifice or get burned, I was the only one who gave up everything I earned.

He said, "I died for you, I cried for you, and this is how you repay it?" It must mean nothin'
that I had a message to convey.
Instead of being a trendsetter, you became an imitator,
and I screamed, "I ain't getting instant gratification, so I'll
see you later!" And I went on trying to discover like I had just hopped off the Mayflower,
trying to play on both sides of the game,
acting like a coward. He said I want you to fear that mean you believe I waved my hand like
whatever and continued trying to leave he allowed me to have it my way besides I was the
only one that had to make the bed where I lay three o'clock that morning I was awakened by
my cousin in my
doorway. He had tears in his eyes, and he wasn't the crying type.
Only thing he could say was, "It's over," and I knew something
wasn't right. Whatever it was, I could tell it was weighing heavy on 'im then he told me my
brother's car ran into a tree and the engine came in on 'im.